Barbara Park

MA!
There's Nothing to Do Here!
A Word from Your Baby-in-Waiting

illustrated by Viviana Garofoli

Random House 🏠 New York

Published in the United States by Random House Children's Books, a division of Random House, Inc., New York.
RANDOM HOUSE and colophon are registered trademarks of Random House, Inc.

www.randomhouse.com/kids

Educators and librarians, for a variety of teaching tools, visit us at www.randomhouse.com/teachers

Library of Congress Cataloging-in-Publication Data
Park, Barbara.
Ma! There's nothing to do here! : a word from your baby-in-waiting / Barbara Park ; illustrations by Viviana Garofoli.
p. cm.
SUMMARY: A baby still waiting to be born describes the boredom of living in a small, cramped space where there are no toys and no
one else can be "it" during a game of tag, then considers how life will change when Baby joins Pop and Ma in the outside world.
ISBN: 978-0-375-83852-1 (trade)
ISBN: 978-0-375-93852-8 (lib. bdg.)
[1. Fetus—Fiction. 2. Babies—Fiction. 3. Stories in rhyme.] I. Garofoli, Viviana, ill. II. Title. III. Title: Ma! There's nothing to do here!
PZ8.3.P1636The 2008
[E]—dc22 2006103326

PRINTED IN CHINA 10 9 8 7 6 5 4 3 2 First Edition

To my sons, Steven and David, who were born in the dark ages before the sonogram.

To my sweet daughter-in-law Renee, who invited me to my first ultrasound (and thus inspired this book!).

And to the *superstars* of the ultrasounds... my two beautiful grandsons, Cal and Nate.

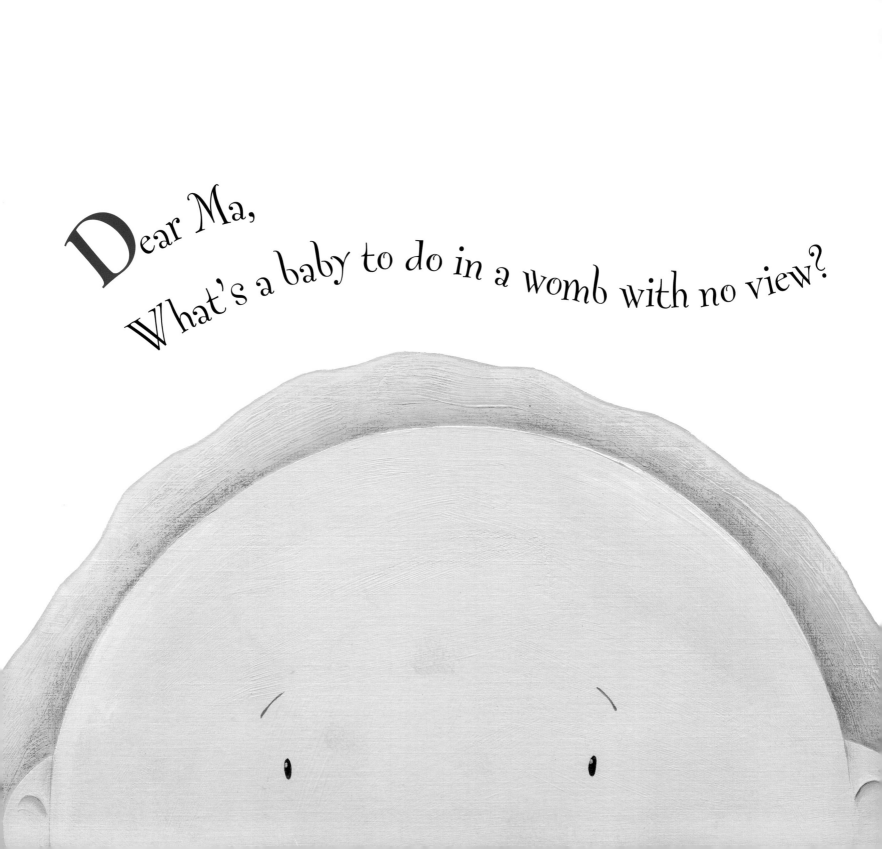

Dear Ma,
What's a baby to do in a womb with no view?

No puppies. No toys.

No girls . . . zero boys.

Not a sandbox or swings . . .

Or those monkey bar things.

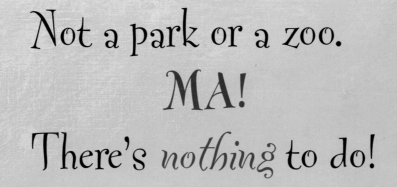

Not a park or a zoo.
MA!
There's *nothing* to do!

My choices are slim.
There is *no* room to swim.
I'm so tired of floating.
I'd love to go boating,
But where's the canoe?
MA!
There's *nothing* to do!

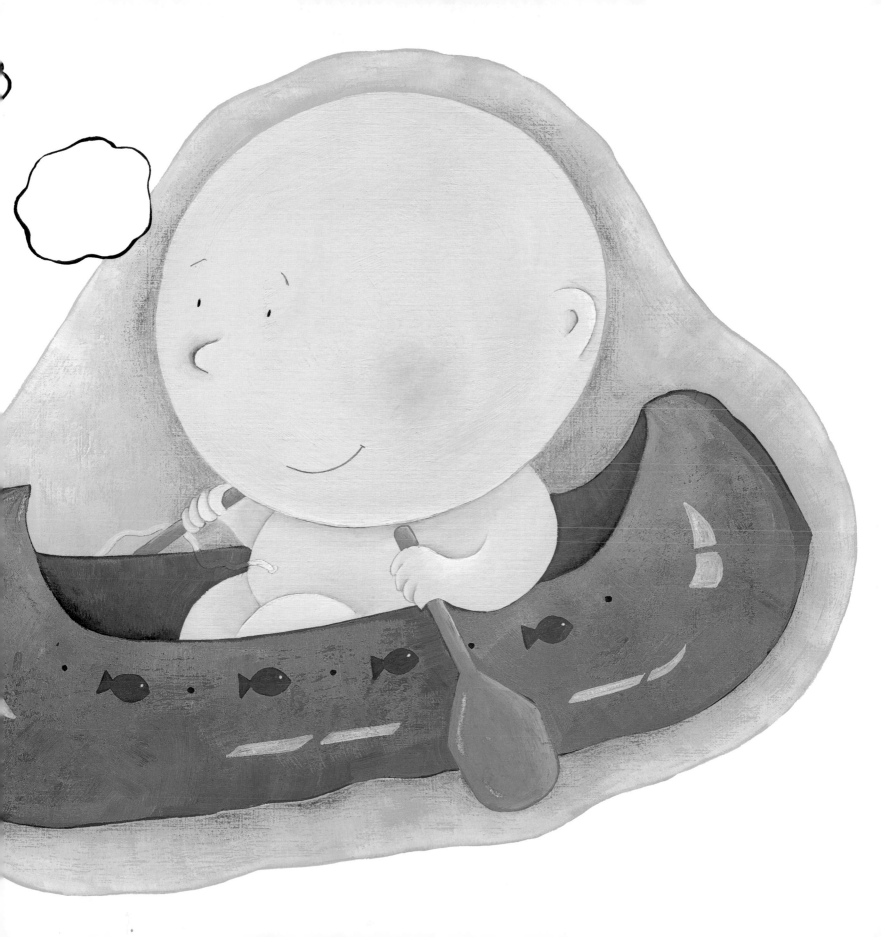

I'm all in a heap here. My feet are asleep here. I'm flat out of space. I've got knees in my face. And I'm totally bored with this dumb bungee cord. . . . I'm NOT kidding you . . . there is NOTHING to do!

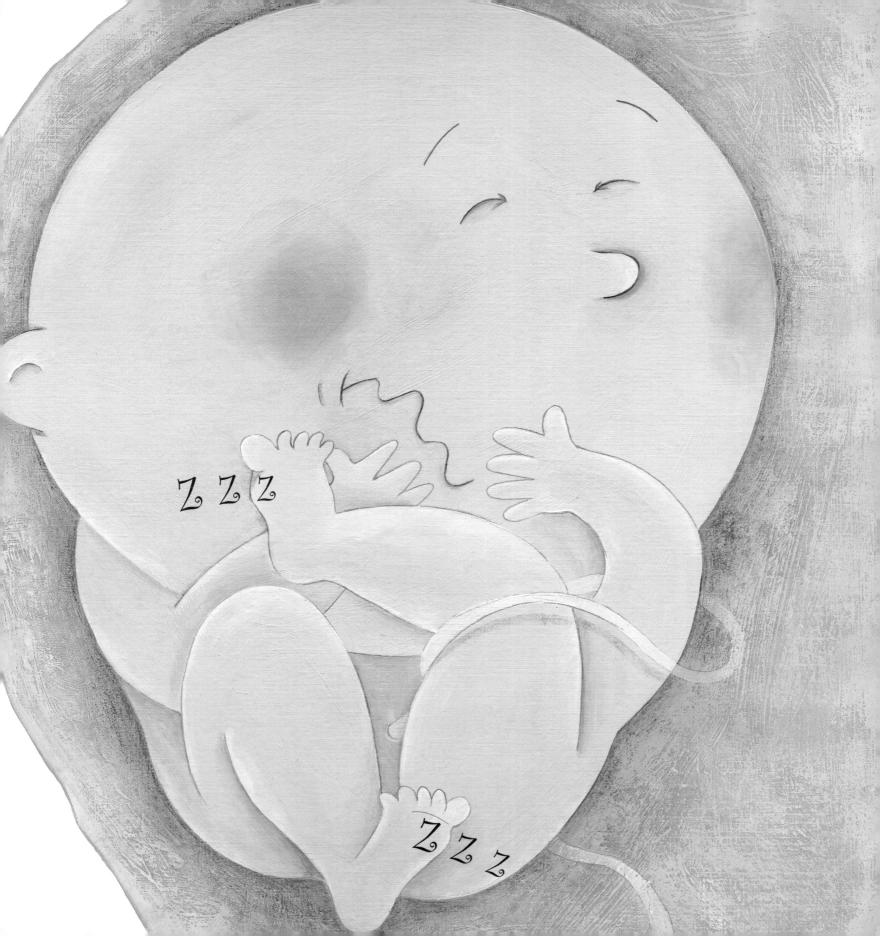

Still . . . I try to stay busy.

I slosh till I'm dizzy.

I practice my kicking.

And hiccup-cup-hicking.

hic

hic hic

hic hic

hic

I'm working on hair. But my head is still bare.

I've tried hide-and-seek and I don't even peek.
But I'm so intertwined, I'm too easy to find.

Plus tag is no fun—I've got no place to run.
And it gives me a fit that I have to stay "IT"!

If I just had a truck.

Or a small rubber duck.

Or a cat or a bug.

Or a teddy named Doug.

'Cause I hear the tick-tock
Of your happy heart clock.
And I bet you a dime
That it's almost

You're set for me, right? You've got a night-light?

mom list :

And diapers? Shampoo?
Does my room have a view?
I could use a good bib.
And I'd like my own crib.

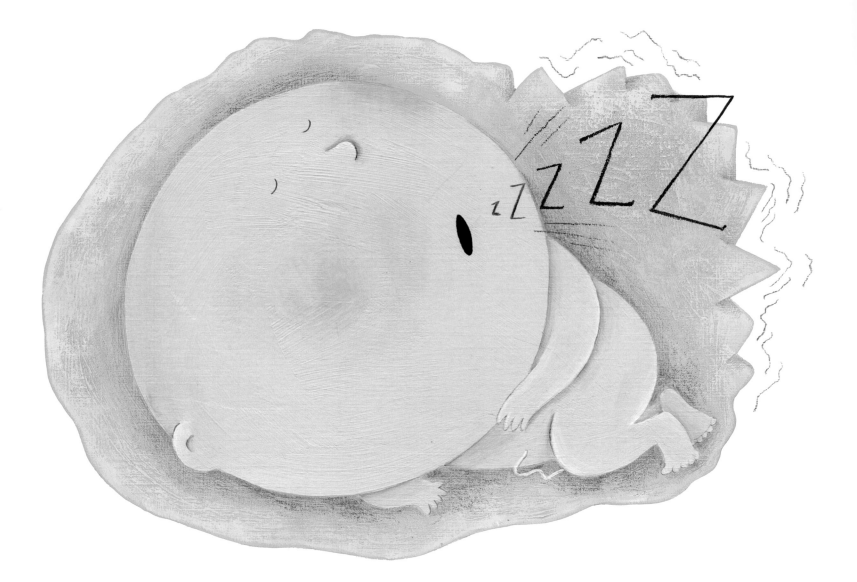

Still—a few worries more:
Ma, I think that I snore.

And nights might get bumpy.
I'll wake, full of grumpy.
And you'll have a hunch
I had grouchies for lunch.

But then, out of the blue,

I will gurgle and coo.

Or I'll wrinkle my nose,

Or discover my toes.

No, wait! I'll grow hair!

WOW!

There's lots to do THERE!

So, Ma, here's the plan.
Let's rest while we can.
I'll stay in here longer—
Get bigger, grow stronger.

Well, that's it, I guess.
I've got your address.
Kiss Pop for me, please . . .
And give him a squeeze.
I'll meet him soon, maybe!

I LOVE YOU,
Your Baby